Welcome to Little Funnies

Little Funnies is a delightful collection of picture books made to put a giggle into storytime.

There are funny stories about a laughing lobster, a daring mouse, a teeny tiny woman, and lots more colourful characters!

Perfect for sharing, these rib-tickling tales will have your little ones coming back for more!

TEE HEE!

HA HA!

*For Oskar, Joe next door
and Tiziana – J.B-B.*

First published 1998 by Walker Books Ltd
87 Vauxhall Walk, London SE11 5HJ

This edition published 2007

10 9 8 7 6 5 4 3 2 1

Text © 1998 Martin Waddell
Illustrations © 1998 John Bendall-Brunello

The moral rights of the author/illustrator have been asserted.

This book has been typeset in Horley.

Printed in China

British Library Cataloguing in Publication Data:
a catalogue record for this book is available from the British Library.

ISBN 978-1-4063-0783-2

www.walkerbooks.co.uk

Yum, Yum, Yummy

Martin Waddell

Illustrated by
John Bendall-Brunello

WALKER BOOKS
AND SUBSIDIARIES

LONDON · BOSTON · SYDNEY · AUCKLAND

One day three little bears went off to the Honey~bee Tree to get honey for Mummy.

Guzzley was there
but the three little bears
didn't see Guzzley Bear.

The three little
bears filled their
pots with honey.
Then they set off
for home.

Greedy Guzzley was there
but the three little bears
didn't see Guzzley Bear.

"*Grr-grr-grr!*"
growled Guzzley Bear.
"Give me your honey!"

Yum, yum, yummy!

The honey went into Guzzley's big tummy.

Three scared little bears ran
all the way home.
"Guzzley Bear stole our honey,"
they told their mummy.
"Don't be scared, little bears,"
said Mummy. "You go for
more honey. I'll see to
that old Guzzley Bear."

The three little bears went
back to the Honey~bee Tree.
Guzzley Bear crept up
behind them. Mummy
was there but
Guzzley Bear
didn't see
Mummy Bear.

"Grr-grr-grr!"
growled Guzzley Bear,
"Give me your honey!"
But out of the
bushes came ...

Mummy!

Guzzley Bear never
came back any more.
The honey went into three
little bear tummies ...

and Mummy's.
Yum,
yum,
yum,
yummy!